PREPARE FOR

PERIL IN THE PEC

SUPER DWEEB VS THE EVIL DOODLER

By Jess Bradley

Mona, my arm's going numb! I can't hold this pose for much longer!

Hang in there! Trust me, it will look really dramatic!

ARCTURUS

BOOKS IN THIS SERIES

1. Super Dweeb and the Pencil of Destiny
2. Super Dweeb Vs Doctor Eraser-Butt
3. Super Dweeb Vs the Evil Doodler
4. Super Dweeb and the Time Trumpet
5. Super Dweeb Vs Count Dorkula
6. Super Dweeb and the Snack Attack

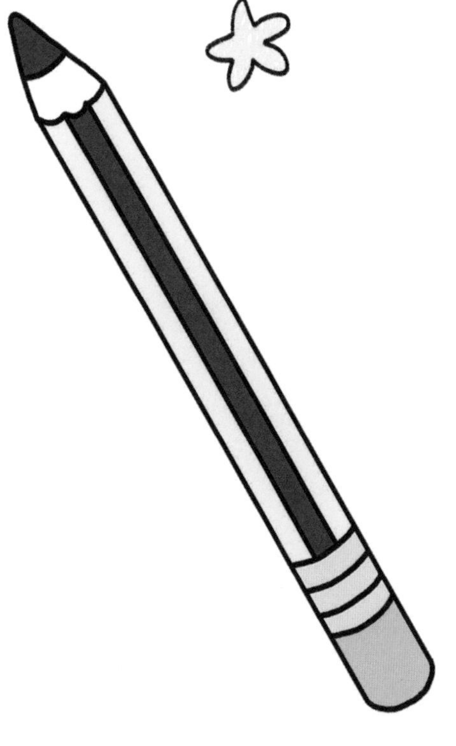

This edition published in 2024 by
Arcturus Publishing Limited
26/27 Bickels Yard, 151–153 Bermondsey Street,
London SE1 3HA

Words and pictures: Jess Bradley
Design: Stefan Holliland
Original concept: Joe Harris

ISBN: 978-1-3988-1910-8
CH007613NT
Supplier 13, Date 0424, PI 00007039

Printed in China

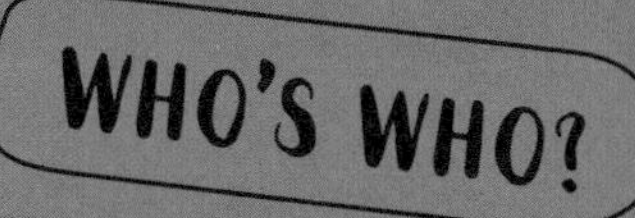

ANDY! Schoolkid and secret superhero

Awesome rating: THE AWESOMEST

MONA! Andy's best friend and tech genius

Awesome rating: ELEVEN OUT OF TEN

OSCAR! Andy's annoying little brother

Awesome rating: NOT VERY

MEAN MIKE! A school bully

Awesome rating: THE EXACT OPPOSITE OF AWESOME

THE PENCIL OF DESTINY!

A radioactive pencil that can bring doodles to life!

Awesome rating: OFF THE SCALE

CONTENTS

Chapter 1 **Keeping Up with the Dweebs**

Hi, everybody! My name is ANDY. Some people say that I'm a DWEEB because I love comics and wear a tie.

On a class trip to a place called Fallout Island, one of my pencils became

RADIOACTIVE

with a substance called Blootonium!

As well as growing in size...

...it brought my doodles to LIFE.

This was all great, until my little bro drew a

RAMPAGING MONSTER!

Brother (Oscar)

My best friend **MONA** talked me into drawing a superhero costume and battling it. I WON!

Because she's so smart, Mona has been offered work experience at A.C.R.O.N.Y.M., a secret spy agency.

I'm glad she can keep an eye on them, because those guys are super shady. One of their scientists even turned into a **SUPERVILLAIN.**

But we rescued his lab monkey, Mr. Sniffles! And Oscar became my sidekick, KID CRAYON!

(Yeah, long story...)

Okay, I think you're up to speed. Now turn the page for

AWESOME SUPERHERO ACTION!

"Andy!" Mr. Squibb shouted, for what I assumed wasn't the first time. Whoops, I was day-dreaming in class again!

You see, I've loved *Gamma Guys* comics ever since I was tiny and now they're ...

"Andy! The whole class is waiting to hear what you think about *Romeo and Juliet!*"

THE WHOLE CLASS → **We're really not...**

"Sorry Mr. Squibb, but the trailer for the GAMMA GUYS movie comes out tomorrow and I just can't concentrate!" I said.

Sigh! Now, as I was saying, it's time to pair up for your diorama project.

Mona is at her internship so I hope I don't get paired with ...

Andy and MIKE!
Nooooo!

Mean Mike is the WORST! He's been the bane of my life since first grade!
* Smug
* Arrogant
* Annoying
* Plays the violin surprisingly well

Ugh, school is terrible without Mona!
Our project title is ...
Dweeb!

... heroes! You will make a diorama based on your own hero!

Gasp!

Gamma Guys!

No way am I doing a nerdy Gamma Guys project.
Aw no ...

Super Dweeb is WAY better!

I have a small and tasteful collection of Super Dweeb merchandise.

Mean Mike's bedroom ...

SUPER DWEEB

Super Dweeb is such a total LEGEND!
Wow!

Why are you smiling, dork?
No reason! I guess he's okay!

"Not all heroes wear capes, you know. Have you considered inspirational figures in your daily lives? A talented TEACHER, for example?"

But I wasn't really listening to Mr. Squibb. Someone called me their <u>H</u> <u>E</u> <u>R</u> <u>O</u>! How cool is that?

Even if it was Mean Mike who liked Super Dweeb, it still made me feel great.

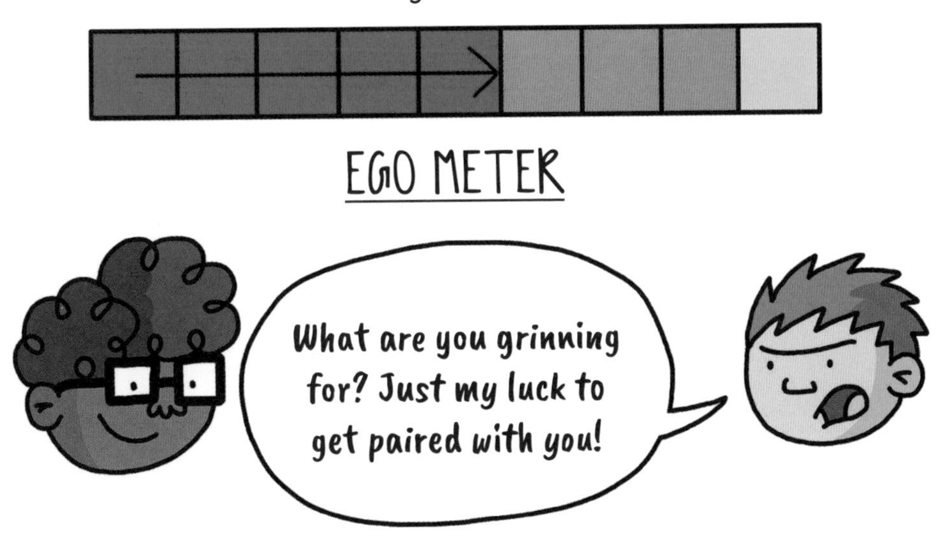

EGO METER
What are you grinning for? Just my luck to get paired with you!

I couldn't wait to tell Mona that I was a <u>class project</u>!

But it's still just school. Nowhere near as cool as ...

SECRET AGENT WORK EXPERIENCE!

Meanwhile at A.C.R.O.N.Y.M., international spy agency ...
Jet pack launch area
Spy training class
Coffee and caviar bar
Soft play area
Zero-gravity spa
Laser watch shooting range
Invisible parking lot

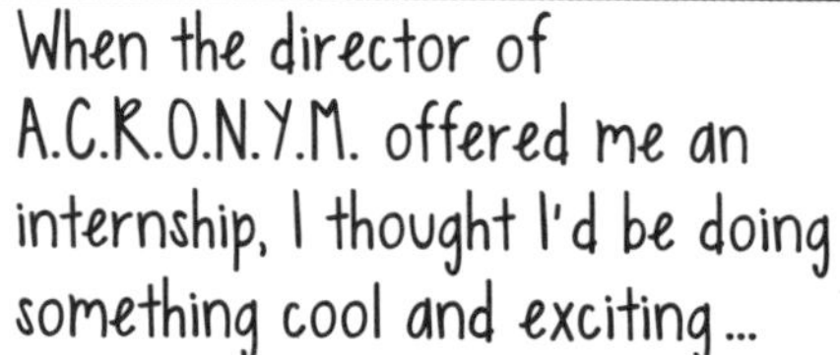
When the director of A.C.R.O.N.Y.M. offered me an internship, I thought I'd be doing something cool and exciting ...

... not just all of the photocopying!

Ugh, I'm so embarrassed!
Beep boop!

Even the coffee-drone gets more respect than me!
Beep!

Hey intern girl! I need you to do some photocopying for me!
Spy guy

I need you to copy everything labelled "Top Secret" but not the stuff that says "Extra Top Secret" okay? But try not to look because you don't have clearance, capiche?
TOP SECRET!
Stop reading right now!
Yes, you! Go away!

How will I know what they say without looking at them??
Use your initiative! Ciao!

How am I meant to ...

What the ...?!

That's Fallout Island! Top secret or not, I need a copy of this!
Beep!

After school, Mona came to my house. My kid brother, Oscar, was hanging out with us, too.
It's time for ...
DUNGEONS & DONUTS
My goblin barista rolls a 20!
I've got 7 sprinkle tokens!
My skeleton is still waiting for his latte, guys.

So, guess who's the subject of a school project?
I give up...

ME! Super Dweeb! I'm a hero!
Okay?

I'm going to be a diorama!
There are worse things to be, I guess!

It's just nice to get some recognition for my work, that's all!
Come on, it's your turn!

Ook ook eek sniff!
Super-smart monkey!
Tater-tot, best dog ever!

Mr. Sniffles says you shouldn't let it go to your head!
I'm pretty sure he just wants more cheese doodles!

Chapter 2 **Too Many Andys**

"Speaking of snacks, looks like we've run out," I said. "Let me just draw something ... !"

"Doodle dupes, would you be so kind as to make me an ULTIMATE SANDWICH?"

Mona frowned. "I don't think making duplicates of yourself is such a great idea."

"But I can get so much more stuff done! They can do my chores, go and visit Grandma, and I can get on with more important things, like waiting for the GAMMA GUYS movie trailer to drop later today!"

Plus, I'm getting really good at this. Don't they look realistic?

Yeek! Gabba!
Wof!
Hmm...

Mr. Sniffles say that you should watch out. No good can come of too many Andys! Tater-Tot agrees.
Okay, Doctor Dolittle!

I have to agree with Oscar, the monkey and the dog. You're making too many doodle dupes! It's kind of weird ...

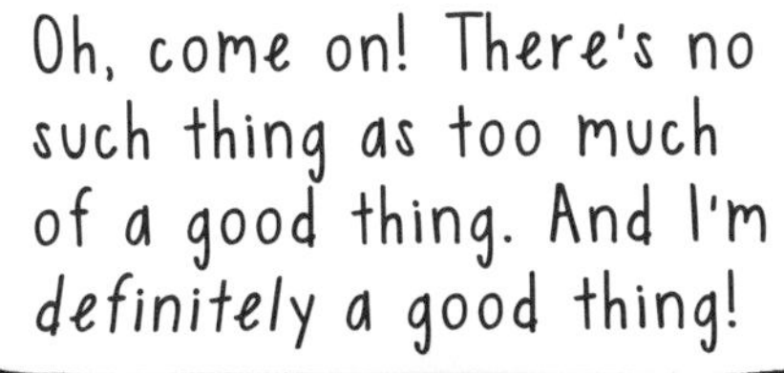

Oh, come on! There's no such thing as too much of a good thing. And I'm *definitely* a good thing!
Watch that ego meter!

GROAN!

"Speaking of a good thing, here comes my ultimate sandwich!

My doodle dupes make it perfectly *EVERY TIME!*"

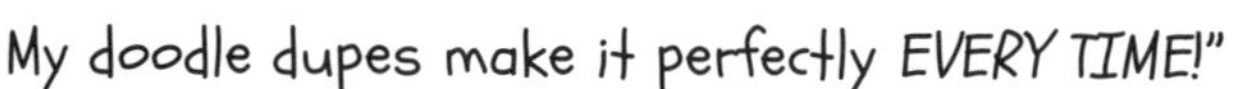

"I feel like that sandwich must be

breaking some kind of law!" said Mona.

"It's so WRONG it must

be RIGHT!" said Oscar.

Munch munch! So how's your work experience going?
Um, yeah! It's great!

Wait, I almost forgot! I was asked to handle some top-secret files. Look at this!

It's Fallout Island, where you got ...
My atomic pencil! Why do A.C.R.O.N.Y.M. have this?

Clearly someone's up to something SNEAKY. Even by super-spy standards!

Ooh, maybe you could spy on the spies?
Ook!*
*Say it, don't spray it!

Yeah, I'll definitely be keeping an eye on them! Me and my new pal, the Coffee Drone 3000!
Beep!

"OOK! SNIFF! OOK!"

said Mr. Sniffles.

"Mr. Sniffles said that you shouldn't be stealing stuff from A.C.R.O.N.Y.M.," translated Oscar. "Their equipment is probably dangerous. Even the water coolers might have missiles!"

"Okay, so firstly I'm just borrowing it so I can upgrade it! Also, it's a coffee drone! How dangerous could it be—"

DEATH MODE ENGAGED!

"NO, *DISENGAGE!* Heh, I need to tinker with it a bit!"

I quietly left Mona and Oscar to go and watch the *Gamma Guys* trailer, FINALLY!

"Mr. Sniffles says you're being a jerk!" said Oscar.

"Can you really understand what he's saying or are *YOU* just calling me a jerk?!"

"We have a special best-friend bond so I can understand him!"

"Fine, fine!" I grumbled. "Let me just go and get into my costume!"

"Gibble gibble!" said Mr. Sniffles.

(Translation: I have a bad feeling about this!)

And so ...

DWEEB SQUAD READY!

Super Dweeb!

Kid Crayon

Mr. Sniffles and Tater-Tot!

"Okay," said Mona, "I've added a new Mona-Mode on the coffee drone so I can come with you in real-time but also stay here and use the computer!"

Can you borrow some other cool tech from A.C.R.O.N.Y.M.? We could equip all of my dupes with awesome spy gadgets!

I've already told you those dupes give me the creeps. I'm not stealing weapons from a spy agency for you!

But you already "borrowed" a coffee drone AND a top secret document ...

CAN WE STOP TALKING ABOUT IT NOW!!
Um, sure!

TO THE DWEEB-MOBILES!

Er, do you mean our scooters?
Sigh. Yes!

Scooters weren't exactly the coolest vehicles, but maybe one day I'd have a JET! Or a CAR! Or even a JET-CAR!

He draws his way out of
trouble! SUPER DWEEB!

Do you need doodles
on the double?
SUPER DWEEB!

He can fix those villains
with a biff and a WHAM!

Something something
something, eating a YAM!!

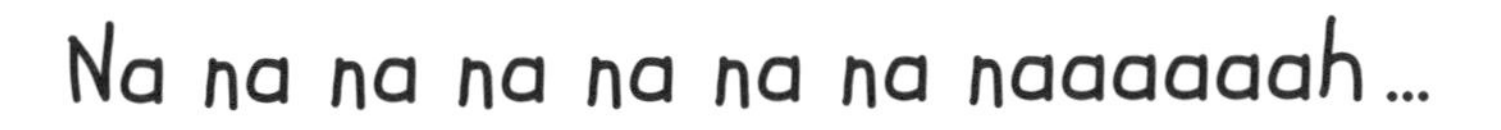

Na na na na na na na naaaaaah...

He's the Super Dweeeeb!

Oscar says: I made this song up when I was in the bathtub!

At the bank ...
That's it. Fill those bags full of money! If you don't do it, I, PAPER GIRL, will get my origami army to slice you to salami!
Gulp
She gave me a papercut!

A paper-themed villain?

How is it even possible to bring paper alive?
Drone vision!

Where did I get my awesome powers, I hear you ask?
Well, I didn't ask, but sure, tell us!

One day at school, I found a bunch of scrap paper with bad drawings on them! When I made an origami bird with them, it came to life!

Andy, do those scrap drawings look familiar to you?

Oh no! Even though drawings that aren't finished don't come to life, it looks like they still have some power!

So the pencil's radiation has more of an effect than I thought! Once the drawings pop out of existence, the paper you drew on is packed with Blootonium radiation!

Ook! Sniff!
He said your carelessness and littering created this mess!

Well, if my pencil created this, it can uncreate it too! GO PENCIL!
Super scribble!

Um...!
Feeble!
Weak!
Heh!
Terrible!
Is it me, or are your drawings a bit worse than usual? They're awful!
Oscar is right! Something's up!

I'll just have to tear apart these paper perils instead!

Ow! Papercut! Papercut!
Swoosh!

Come on, Andy! Get it together!

But my doodles just aren't working properly!

Buhhh!

Bloop!
Fine, plan B! Remember how Mr. Sniffles mentioned dangerous water coolers?

Aha! Water! Paper hates water!
Hoist!

Take this!!
Lob!

Sploosh!

"That didn't go quite how I wanted it to," I grumbled.

The Mona-drone hovered near me. "While I'm VERY concerned that your pencil has a huge effect on paper, I'm more concerned about why it was malfunctioning."

I know, it was almost like my pencil wasn't working properly!

Yeah, Andy, that's what "malfunction" means. I'll run some tests to figure out what's wrong!

This could throw up a whole new set of problems.
Doo doo dee doo!
Tap tap!

Ah, Andy duplicate! Could you just grab me a soda please?
Ha!

I'm ANDY, not a duplicate! HAH! My drawings are so good, you couldn't tell the difference!
Wait, if you're Andy ...

Then who was just fighting Paper Girl?!
Heh! Hello! I'm a doodle duplicate!

YOU SENT A DUPE ANDY OUT TO FIGHT?!
Well, I wanted to stay and watch the Gamma Guys trailer!

Andy, do you realize what you've done?! You created a dupe that has A PENCIL THAT WORKS!!
Not very well, though!

That's not the point!! That dupe is able to draw his own doodles that come to life! This could be really bad!
Mona, he's just a stupid doodle! He'll disappear soon anyway!

That's it! I'm fed up of us dupes having to do the stuff you can't be bothered to do!

We clean and visit Grandma and make endless sandwiches and fight and do we get any thanks for it? NO!

Well, I'm not going to take it anymore! My pencil may not be as powerful, but...
Scribble!

...I can at least draw a get-away rocket!

I have no idea what is happening!
Ook!
Wof!

You know what? I'm better than real Andy in every way! I don't need any of this!!

Whoosh!
Sputter!

Uh, Mona? What do we do now?

Yes, REAL ANDY! What do we do now?!
Heh! Gulp!

Chapter 3 **Bad Times!**

It's safe to say that everyone was REALLY mad at me.

"Well," said Mona through gritted teeth, "this is all basically awful but at least we've found out more about the pencil."

"I'm sure things aren't THAT bad," I said. weakly.

"Andy, you drew a duplicate pencil THAT ACTUALLY WORKED!" said Mona. "And your evil twin was REALLY angry!"

"But surely he'll just pop out of existence, like my other drawings?" I said.

"SCREECH! EEEK! OOK!" gibbered Mr. Sniffles.

"He said you'd better hope that Evil Andy doesn't come back here with an army," Oscar translated.

It's SCIENCE TIME with MONA!

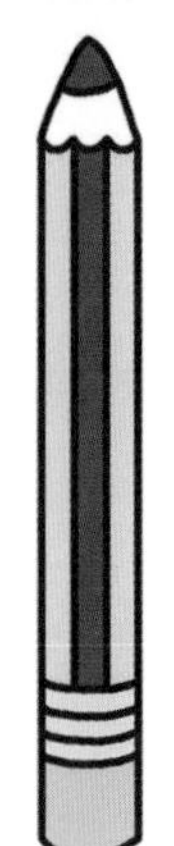

Okay, this is what we know about the atomic pencil so far.

- It makes drawings come to life!
- Drawings last around 10 minutes when they come to life.
- Doodles can feed off graphite to last a bit longer.
- It's **VERY** bad when it falls into the wrong hands.

But the pencil can do other stuff too!

Its eraser shavings have power.

Even paper with leftover doodles on it has radioactive power!

And the pencil can draw other pencils that work!

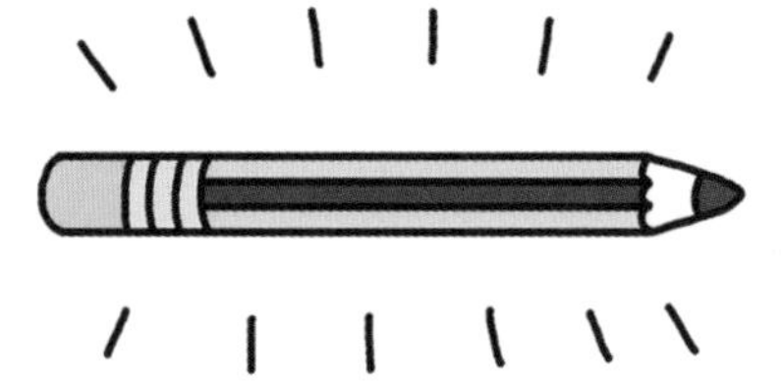

"So now another version of Andy has an atomic pencil too!"

"He won't come back with an army!" I stuttered nervously.

"Let's just hope he doesn't find any graphite up in space before he pops out of existence," Mona said. "He was really angry at you, and I can't blame him!"

"And your pencil is getting blunt too!" said Oscar. "You're in trouble if he **DOES** come back for revenge!"

"He's going to come back with an army!!" I shrieked. "We have to prepare!!"

"I need to draw! I need to make my own army!"

Sputter!
Creak!

My ship is destabilizing! I need to find fuel!

I need to find a source of graphite, otherwise I'll cease to exist, like Super Idiot's other drawings!
Grr! The NERVE of him!

Grr, Original Andy will pay for thinking he's the best!

I'll show them all who's the best!
ME!!
It's ME!!
Stomp!

Aha! There's a space port!

Hey Alien Guy! Do you sell pencils?
!!!

Pencils? You mean drawing sticks?

No, we don't, sorry!

Gah! I need to find graphite!
Oh, graphite!

If it's graphite you're after, that passing meteor is MADE of it!

Dramatic music!
Yessss! Thank you, Alien Guy!

Time to set up shop on that meteor... !
Bye!

HA!

GRAPHITE!
Nom!

Now I have ALL THE POWER!!!
EGO METER OVERLOAD!

After eating all this graphite, my doodle army will be unstoppable!
EVIL SCRIBBLES!

Time to ditch this lame costume too. I need something a bit more edgy.
EVIL FASHION SCRIBBLES!

Watch out, Super Dweeb! I'm coming for you! We ALL ARE!

Chapter 4 **The Temple of Gloom**

"Wait, Andy," Mona said. "I think I've worked out what's going on! The NEW pencil is draining power from the ORIGINAL one. That's why it won't work properly anymore."

"HOW DO WE FIX IT?!" I cried.

Mona pulled a piece of paper out of her pocket. "Remember this top-secret document I found at A.C.R.O.N.Y.M.? It looks like there's a pencil sharpener on this other island!"

It's all written in code but that won't stop me!
Hacker Time!

If I can just crack the passcode, I'll be able to access A.C.R.O.N.Y.M.'s secret code spreadsheet!
They keep all their codes in a spreadsheet?!
YUP.

Now, if I upload the map and interface the code document with it we should ...
A

Hey presto! It's decoded!
Hey, that's Fallout Island, where my pencil was transformed!

And just to the north of it there's an island with a mysterious temple containing a mystic pencil sharpener!
That's weirdly convenient!

There's even a picture of it!

"It looks like whatever the sharpener is, it's in some kind of temple on this other island," said Mona.

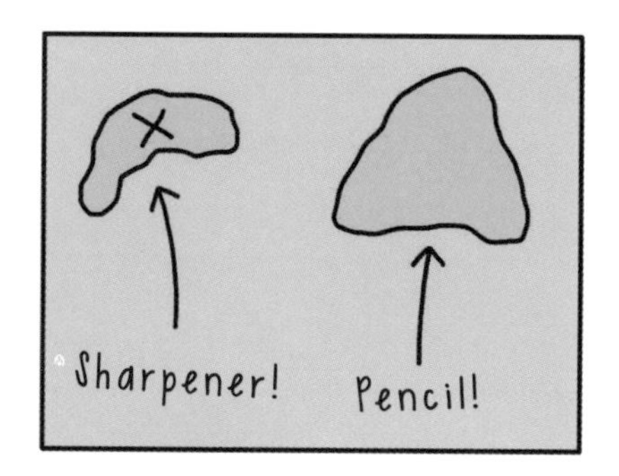

"How come you didn't know about this if you were handling top-secret documents?" I asked.

"I ... uh ... well ... gah! The truth is, I'm just a glorified photocopier! My internship is not as good as I thought it would be. I didn't want to tell you because I was embarrassed," Mona said.

"Mona, you're the smartest person I know and you're awesome! I don't care about how terrible your internship is. LOOK WHAT YOU FOUND!"

Mona grinned. "Thanks Andy! We'll talk about this more tomorrow. For now, we need a plan! I propose this: I'll take Mr. Sniffles and Tater-Tot and find this sharpener. You and Oscar get ready for the evil doodler and distract him until I get back!"

"Maybe if we feed Andy's wobbly drawings normal pencils they'll last longer!" said Oscar.

WE HAD A PLAN!

At the docks ...
Captain Poopdeck!

Hello there, weird girl I met in a previous adventure!

We need to get to this island as fast as possible! Could you take us?

Oh, so it's Secondary Plot Device Island ye be seeking! Yar, I can take ye! But first ...

"You find nothing but HORROR on Secondary Plot Device Island! Horror!!"
A HUGE snapping turtle!
"En garde!"
Whatever the heck this thing is!
Giant spiders trained in swordsmanship!
A bear with a grudge!
An annoying king who will make you search for a baby in a maze!
A stop for a bus that is always late!
Lots of other stuff!!
I really don't have time for this. Couldn't we just go around the other side?

Yar, I hadn't thought of that! I'll just sail you to the other side of the island! You'll skip all of that nonsense and go straight to the temple!

Yeek! Gabble!
I agree! Why didn't he just say that in the first place?

Come aboard! I've got a new waffle machine!

And so ...
Nearly there! So why are you going to that island?

Oh, just trying to locate some kind of relic, that's all!

Oh, look! There it be!
Woah!

Mysterious music plays ...

Here you go! I'll wait on the boat and do some sudoku!
Thank you!

Okay guys, let's check this out!

Wow, this is awesome!

Erk! Uh, maybe not so awesome.

Yeek!

That's very convenient! A little *too* convenient.

Well, there it is! I guess I'll just ... take it?
More dramatic music!

Oh, okay! This is good! No booby traps!

I guess there was nothing to worry about after all! Phew! That was lucky!
KA-BOOM!!

We're done, Captain Poopdeck!

Did I ever tell you about the time I hitched a ride on a giant squid?

Wait, what's that on Fallout Island?

Zoom

Argh! A.C.R.O.N.Y.M.!
A.C.R.O.N.Y.M

Hopefully, this won't come back to haunt us in the next story!
Click!

We need to get back to Andy, quick!

Chapter 5 **Andy V Anti-Andy**

Back at Andy's house ...

"Uh, I think your EVIL TWIN is coming!" said Oscar.

"These are all the normal pencils I can find. We'll feed them to my doodles and hope the graphite keeps them going!"

Come on, Andy! We can do this! No evil clone can defeat us! Especially if he's as dumb as you are!

"RUDE!" I said. "But I get your point, Oscar— LET'S DO THIS!"

I'm better than you in every way! And my Andy Army are going to kick your behind!

Andy
Power-ometer
Doodle slap!
Keep feeding my doodles, Oscar!
Carrot kung fu kick!
Panda power!

EVIL
Power-ometer
Andy
Anti-Andy ants, attack!
Kick received!
Ha! Your doodles are terrible!
Bear battle begin!

We need some kind of distraction!

Can you make the perfect Ultimate Sandwich, then?

OF COURSE I CAN! I USED TO MAKE ANDY'S SANDWICHES ALL THE TIME!

Sure you did. But were they really "ultimate?"
Simmering rage!

GET ME SANDWICH FIXINGS!! RIGHT NOW!!

Oscar, you're a genius! His ego is so fragile, he can't resist the challenge!

Come on, Mona!

And so ...
Gentlemen, please present your sandwiches! I, Oscar, will judge by eating said sandwiches!

Andy, your sandwich!

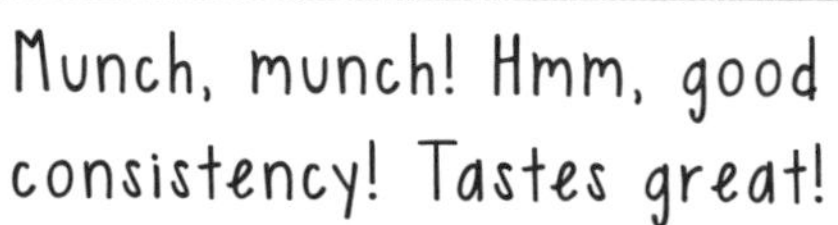
Munch, munch! Hmm, good consistency! Tastes great!

Now, Evil Andy. If you will!

Mmm, a good amount of mustard! Love that extra chip crunch!

Hmm, I think we need to have a round 2 to be sure!

Wait a sec! This is just a distraction!
Scribble!

No more games!

Gulp! I can't draw anything! We'll get smooshed!

Hey! Mr. Sniffles!
Ook!*
*surprise

ANDY! Heads up!
HEY! What's that?

YES!!
Catch!

Sharpen!

Ha ha! My pencil is sharper than ever!
Scribble!

Let's go!

STOP HITTING YOURSELF!
NOOOO!

Yes! Your robot is trashing his and his doodle army is disappearing!
Pop!
Pop!
Pop!

Pop!
Snatch!
Hey!

Snap!!
Power broken!
Noooooo!

In your face, Evil Andy!

It's not fair! I didn't want to be evil! I just wanted to not be a glorified waiter all the time!

I just wanted to be able to play Dungeons and Donuts too! And watch the *Gamma Guys* trailer!

Oh no! Now I feel really guilty! Like, *really* guilty!
Sigh! Of course you do!

"THIS IS ALL MY FAULT!" I said. "I've turned a fellow dweeb into a monster! My ego got the better of me!"

"Why couldn't we have just teamed up?" said Evil Andy.

Like in issue #251 of *Gamma Guys*!

I'm sorry, doodle Andy! I won't make any more duplicates!

Unless we get to help you too!

Deal!

See you soon!
Phew! I'm glad that's all sorted!

Pop!

"Well," said Mona, "While I'm sure all of that could have been avoided, things worked out!"

"I've learned a valuable lesson, too!" I said.

"Not to take your doodles for granted?" asked Oscar.

"Uh, that too! But also that we should probably leave before we get blamed for the huge meteor over there! Let's go!"

"Yeep!" said Mr. Sniffles.

Back at Mona's, we were ready to get back into our game of Dungeons and Donuts ...

I think we need to keep an eye on A.C.R.O.N.Y.M.! They've found Fallout Island and they're up to something!

"Are you going to quit your internship, Mona?" I asked.

"No," said Mona. "I'm going to work from the inside! I'll keep photocopying and pretend not to know anything! They'll never suspect me."

Like a real spy! Awesome!

Even better— a spy who spies on spies.

"You know, we have a pretty good team here! We've got a Super Dweeb ..."

"A secret agent!"

"A sidekick!"

"A monkey!"

"And a dog!"

"And I will go and get us some awesome snacks all by myself, with no help from my doodles!" I said.

"Just *one thing*, Andy," said Mona.

"Please don't make us an

ULTIMATE SANDWICH,

though. It just looks gross."

"I actually really liked it!" said Oscar.

Three hours later ...
Yes! +6 sprinkle points!
Not if my dragon rolls a 5! I'll trap you in my donut dungeon!
I'd like to see you try!
A 5! Ha ha ha!
GAH!!
FIN!